**HOPSCOTCH
FAIRY TALES**

Jack
and the
Beanstalk

First published in 2007 by
Franklin Watts
338 Euston Road
London
NW1 3BH

Franklin Watts Australia
Level 17/207 Kent Street
Sydney
NSW 2000

A CIP catalogue record for this book is available
from the British Library.

ISBN 978 0 7496 7078 8 (hbk)
ISBN 978 0 7496 7422 9 (pbk)

Series Editor: Melanie Palmer
Series Advisor: Dr Barrie Wade
Series Designer: Peter Scoulding

Printed in China

Franklin Watts is a division of Hachette Children's Books.

Jack
and the
Beanstalk

by Anne Adeney and Tim Archbold

FRANKLIN WATTS
LONDON•SYDNEY

Long ago, there lived a poor boy
named Jack. He sold milk from
his cow, Milky-white.

5

One day, Milky-white had
no milk left.
"You must sell her at the
market," said Mother.

On the way to the market, Jack met an old man. He told Jack: "I'll swap these magic beans for your cow. They will make you rich!"

Jack took the beans and ran home.
"I've swapped Milky-white for
some magic beans!" he said.

"You stupid boy!" shouted Mother, throwing the beans out of the window. "Now we will starve."

Jack woke up hungry. Outside his window he saw a huge beanstalk. "The beans were magic!" he cried.

The beanstalk reached high into
the sky. Jack climbed up and up.

At the top of the beanstalk, Jack saw
a huge castle and a giantess. The
kind giantess gave Jack some food.

Suddenly there was a loud crash.

"That's my husband," she said.

"Quick, hide!"

14

"**Fe fi fo fum**, I smell the blood of an Englishman! Be he alive or be he dead, I'll grind his bones to make my bread!" roared the giant. "Nonsense! You smell the cow I cooked for breakfast," said his wife.

After breakfast, the giant counted
his gold. Soon he fell asleep.
Jack quietly snatched the gold.

Then Jack raced home. Mother
was delighted and they lived
richly for weeks.

Soon, Jack climbed up the
beanstalk again.

"My husband was angry about
his gold," said the giantess.

Jack heard the giant coming
and hid in the oven.

"**Fe fi fo fum**, I smell ..."

"Fiddlesticks! You smell the sheep
I stewed for lunch," said his wife.

After lunch, the giant got out
a hen and ordered:
"Lay, hen, lay!"
The hen laid a golden egg.

Soon the giant was snoring. Jack grabbed the hen and dashed for the beanstalk.

"This hen will lay golden eggs
for us, Mother," said Jack.
"We will never starve again."

Later, Jack wondered how the
giantess was. He climbed up
the beanstalk again.

"You are brave to come back," said the giantess. "My husband could eat you in one mouthful! Quick, hide in here!"

"**Fe fi fo fum ...**" roared the giant.
"Silly giant! The only thing you smell is the pig I've roasted for supper," said his wife.

After supper, the giant took out
a golden harp to play a tune.
"Play, harp, play!" he ordered. The
harp played until the giant slept.

26

Jack seized the harp and ran.

But the harp cried out:

"I am stolen, Master!"

The angry giant woke up
and chased Jack down the
beanstalk. Jack hurried down
as fast as he could and yelled:
"Quick, Mother, get me an axe!"

As the giant roared with rage, Jack chopped down the beanstalk.

The giant was never seen
again and everyone lived
happily ever after.

Hopscotch has been specially designed to fit the requirements of the National Literacy Strategy. It offers real books by top authors and illustrators for children developing their reading skills. There are 43 Hopscotch stories to choose from:

Marvin, the Blue Pig
ISBN 978 0 7496 4619 6

Plip and Plop
ISBN 978 0 7496 4620 2

The Queen's Dragon
ISBN 978 0 7496 4618 9

Flora McQuack
ISBN 978 0 7496 4621 9

Willie the Whale
ISBN 978 0 7496 4623 3

Naughty Nancy
ISBN 978 0 7496 4622 6

Run!
ISBN 978 0 7496 4705 6

The Playground Snake
ISBN 978 0 7496 4706 3

"Sausages!"
ISBN 978 0 7496 4707 0

The Truth about Hansel and Gretel
ISBN 978 0 7496 4708 7

Pippin's Big Jump
ISBN 978 0 7496 4710 0

Whose Birthday Is It?
ISBN 978 0 7496 4709 4

The Princess and the Frog
ISBN 978 0 7496 5129 9

Flynn Flies High
ISBN 978 0 7496 5130 5

Clever Cat
ISBN 978 0 7496 5131 2

Moo!
ISBN 978 0 7496 5332 3

Izzie's Idea
ISBN 978 0 7496 5334 7

Roly-poly Rice Ball
ISBN 978 0 7496 5333 0

I Can't Stand It!
ISBN 978 0 7496 5765 9

Cockerel's Big Egg
ISBN 978 0 7496 5767 3

How to Teach a Dragon Manners
ISBN 978 0 7496 5873 1

The Truth about those Billy Goats
ISBN 978 0 7496 5766 6

Marlowe's Mum and the Tree House
ISBN 978 0 7496 5874 8

Bear in Town
ISBN 978 0 7496 5875 5

The Best Den Ever
ISBN 978 0 7496 5876 2

ADVENTURE STORIES

Aladdin and the Lamp
ISBN 978 0 7496 6678 1 *
ISBN 978 0 7496 6692 7

Blackbeard the Pirate
ISBN 978 0 7496 6676 7 *
ISBN 978 0 7496 6690 3

George and the Dragon
ISBN 978 0 7496 6677 4 *
ISBN 978 0 7496 6691 0

Jack the Giant-Killer
ISBN 978 0 7496 6680 4 *
ISBN 978 0 7496 6693 4

TALES OF KING ARTHUR

1. The Sword in the Stone
ISBN 978 0 7496 6681 1 *
ISBN 978 0 7496 6694 1

2. Arthur the King
ISBN 978 0 7496 6683 5 *
ISBN 978 0 7496 6695 8

3. The Round Table
ISBN 978 0 7496 6684 2 *
ISBN 978 0 7496 6697 2

4. Sir Lancelot and the Ice Castle
ISBN 978 0 7496 6685 9 *
ISBN 978 0 7496 6698 9

TALES OF ROBIN HOOD

Robin and the Knight
ISBN 978 0 7496 6686 6 *
ISBN 978 0 7496 6699 6

Robin and the Monk
ISBN 978 0 7496 6687 3 *
ISBN 978 0 7496 6700 9

Robin and the Friar
ISBN 978 0 7496 6688 0 *
ISBN 978 0 7496 6702 3

Robin and the Silver Arrow
ISBN 978 0 7496 6689 7 *
ISBN 978 0 7496 6703 0

FAIRY TALES

The Emperor's New Clothes
ISBN 978 0 7496 7077 1 *
ISBN 978 0 7496 7421 2

Cinderella
ISBN 978 0 7496 7073 3 *
ISBN 978 0 7496 7417 5

Snow White
ISBN 978 0 7496 7074 0 *
ISBN 978 0 7496 7418 2

Jack and the Beanstalk
ISBN 978 0 7496 7078 8 *
ISBN 978 0 7496 7422 9

The Three Billy Goats Gruff
ISBN 978 0 7496 7076 4 *
ISBN 978 0 7496 7420 5

The Pied Piper of Hamelin
ISBN 978 0 7496 7075 7 *
ISBN 978 0 7496 7419 9

* hardback